ANDY DAY

Illustrated by
STEVEN LENTON

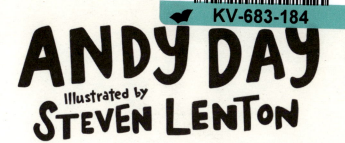

DINO DAD

PUFFIN

PUFFIN BOOKS

UK | USA | Canada | Ireland | Australia
India | New Zealand | South Africa

Puffin Books is part of the Penguin Random House group of companies
whose addresses can be found at global.penguinrandomhouse.com.

www.penguin.co.uk   www.puffin.co.uk   www.ladybird.co.uk

First published 2024
001

Text copyright © Andy Day, 2024
Illustrations copyright © Steven Lenton, 2024

The moral right of the author and illustrator has been asserted

Set in Bembo Infant MT Std
Text design by Sam Combes
Printed in Great Britain by Clays Ltd, Elcograf S.p.A.

A CIP catalogue record for this book is available from the British Library

ISBN: 978–0–241–64292–4

PUFFIN BOOKS

DINO DAD

To Spencer
Have a Roarsome read
Love Andy x

and

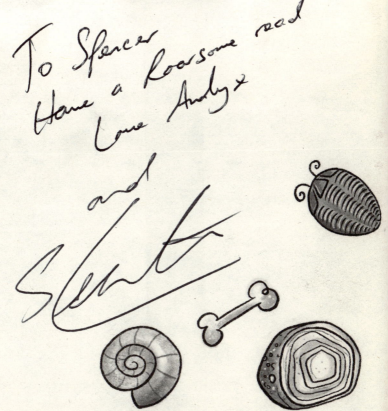

For my beautiful, funny
and cheeky girls —
Ruby-Roo and Indiana.
A.D.

Welcome to Dinotropolis,
Oscar August Toime!
Love, S.L. X

Hi! My name's Ruby Thumb.

I'm six-and-a-little-bit years old, and I have long, wavy blonde hair. I love outdoor adventures, solving problems and learning new things. Oh, and dinosaurs – you'll soon see why!

I live on a very NORMAL street, in a very NORMAL house, where EVERYTHING is absolutely and completely **NORMAL**...

(Pssst – I have to say that because Dad told me to. Thanks to our Big Secret, we're actually totally NOT NORMAL . . . but I'll tell you about that soon, I promise!)

This is my mum, Belinda Thumb.

She is kind, caring and very hard-working, and she makes super-delicious dinners (her

blue-coconut curry is my favourite). When she's not looking after me and my sister (and my dad, she says), Mum works as a photographer. She travels all around the world taking pictures of rare animals.

OOOPS – I shouldn't have shown you that last one! Erm, let me introduce you to my little sister instead . . .

ROAR!

Her real name is Indiana, but we call her 'Little Indie'. She's SO much fun, super cute and always on the move. She can't speak yet, but she can ROAR! Dad says, 'Since your sister was born, I've doubled in age', which doesn't make sense if you ask me, because he still only has one birthday a year.

HAPPY BIRTHDA DAD!

And this is my dad, Lionel Thumb – otherwise known as Dino Dad!

Dad is super tall, with big, curly hair and a huge smile! He says he is sooo tall that he can high-five the moon, which is silly, of course – the moon doesn't have hands!

Dad **REALLY** LOVES DINOSAURS. In fact, he's a dinosaur expert! He owns

5

THUMB'S PREHISTORIC MUSEUM of WONDER

a VERY popular local
dinosaur museum, full of fossils and
models of amazing prehistoric creatures
that people come from all over the world
to visit. There's not a THING my dad
doesn't know about dinosaurs – and you
could say it runs in the family.

You see, my great–great-**GREAT**-
grandad, William Thumb, named the
first-ever dinosaur to be discovered – the
Megalosaurus. So it's no surprise that
Dad is an expert (well, that's not the
only reason ... I'll get to that soon,
promise!)

 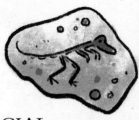

Dad also keeps a very SPECIAL
collection of fossils in his study at
home, where he spends A LOT of his
time working. The door is always locked,
and we're not allowed to go in there.
EXCEPT sometimes on very
special 'Dino-Dad Days'!

Dino-Dad Day is always
on a Saturday – usually when
Mum goes to work. Dad looks
after me and Indie for the WHOLE DAY,

 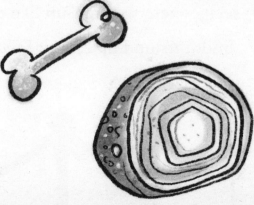

and we always do all sorts of amazing dinosaur-y things!

We go to the museum, fossil hunting, and we even play dinosaur hide-and-seek, where we dress up like our favourite dinosaurs and hide, then Dad comes to find us.

And SOMETIMES Dad opens up his study and lets me and Indie see all the super old and really cool prehistoric artefacts he has in there.

Dad's favourite fossil is a shell full of all the colours of the rainbow. It's called an ammonite shell, and Dad says we

must never touch it, because it's VERY
SPECIAL and VERY, **VERY** RARE.

Of course, back before our first
adventure, I didn't know just how super
special it really was!

It all started a little while ago, on a
Dino-Dad Day I'll never forget . . .

Chapter 1
WHERE'S LITTLE INDIE?

'It's Dino-Dad Day!' Mum sang, as she drew the curtains in my room, letting the sunshine beam in.

'*ROAR, ROAR!*' Little Indie yelled, wriggling in Mum's arms.

I was so excited that I leapt out of bed, which made Little Indie laugh as she thought I was chasing her.

'Sorry, Indie,' I said through my giggles. 'I've got to get dressed!'

'*Roar,*' she replied disappointedly.

I ran to my dressing-up box and looked inside – there were T.rex, Argentinosaurus, Maiasaura and Troodon costumes. Basically all of my favourite dinosaurs!

'You'll need to be quick, Ruby,' said Mum. 'I'm off to work in five minutes, and I hear Dino Dad has got a lot planned for you today. In fact, he mentioned something about –' she paused and smiled – 'unlocking his study?'

'**Wwwhhhattttt??**' I screeched in delight. 'YAY!'

'*Roar, roar!*' Little Indie sounded as excited as me!

I looked at my costumes again. 'I choose . . . the mighty T.rex!' It had

12

a BIG HEAD and TINY ARMS and big **STOMPY** feet, so when I'd got it on, naturally I jumped up to CHASE Mum and Indie down the stairs.

STOMP, STOMP! I pounded my feet on the ground. 'ROAR, I'm a scary T.rex! And I'm HUNGRY!' I shouted.

I was just about to catch them when . . .
'**ROARRRRR**, got ya!'

Something grabbed me and swung me
over its shoulder! Then it started tickling
me – was it a monster? Was it a tickling
robot programmed to make me fall over
in a fit of laughter? NO! It had to be
DINO DAD!

'Good morning, my little dino divas!'

'Ha ha haaaaaa! DAD, put me DOWN!' I said, laughing.

Dad put me back on the ground – and I started laughing again when I saw what he was wearing. Dad was dressed in a very tight and far too short Velociraptor costume – he looked ridiculous!

Mum gave him A Look.

'I know, I know,' he said. 'It shrunk in the wash! But it is TECHNICALLY more accurate now. Did you know that Velociraptors were actually only about the size of chickens, kids?'

16

I giggled. 'You're the biggest chicken I've ever seen, Dad!!'

'*Bo cuuuk!*' He clucked and flapped his arms.

'Hmm, yes.' Mum chuckled. 'Well, I'm off! See you later – and Ruby, it's your favourite for tea tonight.'

'Blue-coconut curry?!' I gasped. I LOVE Mum's special curry!

'You've got it!' she said, kissing me goodbye on the head.

It's the blue coconuts in the curry that make it extra yummy! 'It's a secret Thumb-family ingredient, Ruby Roo,' Mum says. I did wonder why my friends had never heard of BLUE coconuts, though – they are REALLY missing out!

'Goodbye, dear wife! You are the dressing to my salad,' Dad said, swooping in to give Mum a big kiss and take Little Indie from her.

'Get off, you big tree!' Mum laughed. 'Bye, girls! See you later!'

Once Mum was out of the door, Dad turned to us.

'OK, my little prehistoric pea pods! Are

18

you ready for some DINO-DAD FUN?!'

'YEAH!' I yelled.

'*ROAR,*' shouted Indie. But
as soon as Dad put her down,
she shot into the kitchen.

'Indie! Come back!'
Dad zipped after her, and

I skipped into the kitchen behind them.
Dad was chasing Indie, bashing his
Velociraptor head on the ceiling light as
he ran laps round the table.

'**OUCH** – Little Indie – OUCH –
come back – OUCH!'

Luckily for Dad, I knew just what
to do. I picked up Indie's favourite toy –
her Roary the Roaring Nursery-
Rhyme Dino – and pressed its claw to
turn it on.

'*ROAR, ROAR, RROAR, ROAR,
ROAR, RROAR . . .*' As soon
as it played her favourite
nursery rhyme, Indie
immediately stopped
running, and started

wiggling her baby
bum to the beat.

'Works every
time.' I smiled.

'Phew – thanks, Ruby!'
said Dad, who was out of
breath. He quickly scooped
Indie up and plonked her into her
highchair. I sat down at the kitchen table,
too – and then I noticed the volcano.

'Ooooh, what's this, Dino Dad?'

'Ta-da! It's my prehistoric porridge!'
Dad beamed. 'I made it last night.
Watch this!'

Dad picked up a jug of bright-red
porridge and poured it into the model
volcano. It filled up . . . and then, with

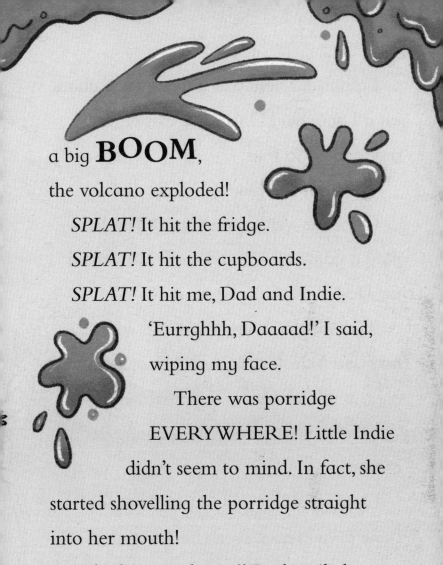

a big **BOOM**,
the volcano exploded!

SPLAT! It hit the fridge.

SPLAT! It hit the cupboards.

SPLAT! It hit me, Dad and Indie.

'Eurrghhh, Daaaad!' I said,
wiping my face.

There was porridge
EVERYWHERE! Little Indie
didn't seem to mind. In fact, she
started shovelling the porridge straight
into her mouth!

'Oh, dinosaur bones!' Dad wailed.
'Sorry, girls. Ruby, you take Indie to get
cleaned up while I sort this out . . .'

I giggled. There was always some chaos on a Dino-Dad Day. That was what made them so fun!

'No problem, Dad. Come on, Indie!'

Once we were cleaned up, I decided to play a game with Indie while we waited for Dad.

'Let's play hide-and-seek! I'll count, and you hide. Ready . . .?' I closed my eyes, and heard Indie scamper away.

'. . . seven, eight, nine, ten – coming, ready or not!'

I looked all around but couldn't find Indie anywhere. I even checked the toilet – she'd managed to fall in once, and I didn't want that to happen again!

Then, just as I was walking back

towards the kitchen, I stopped. Dad's study door was UNLOCKED and OPEN.

Oh no!

'Indie! You know you can't go in there!' We'd be in so much trouble if Dad found out about this.

All of a sudden, I heard Little Indie say, '*Roar, roar, ROAR!*' followed by a loud rumbling . . . and then a FLASH of light burst out of the room!

What WAS that?

I stomped through the door as fast as I could and looked around. On the floor, I could see Dad's VERY RARE and VERY SPECIAL ammonite shell. *Ooh, he is not going to be happy about that,* I thought . . . but also, there was no sign of Little Indie **ANYWHERE!**

Chapter 2
POOPAS

Where was she?! *She can't have gone far*, I thought.

I tried to pick up the ammonite shell and put it back on Dad's table. But it was really HEAVY – weirdly heavy!

I looked around. Dad's study was HUGE and filled with lots of amazing dinosaur artefacts. There were also loads of really old books on a shelf shaped like a Diplodocus, and on the wall were

photos of my relatives through the
generations – right up to Dino Dad.
I noticed that they were all holding the
special ammonite shell in their hands.
Maybe that was why Dad loved it
so much?

'Indiana . . . come out now!' I said.

I'm good at solving problems, so I
thought there were only three things that
could have happened to Indie:

1. She was REALLY good at hiding,
and I just hadn't found her yet.

2. She'd been beamed up by aliens
and was helping them understand the
mind of a baby.

3. She had exploded in a giant ball of
toddler energy.

Hmm, I thought. *It must be option one, although option two is VERY possible.*

Suddenly, I heard Dad calling from the kitchen.

'Ruby Roo! Little Indie! Where have you got to? Time for an adventure!'

Uh oh. I knew we'd be in trouble for being in his study, but I had to tell him what had happened.

'DINO DAD!' I yelled. 'IN HERE!'

Dino Dad rushed through the office
door, hitting his Velociraptor head as
he entered.

'Oww!' he said, and took it off. 'Ruby?
Why are you in my study? You know
you're not allowed
in here.'

Then Dad looked
down and was shocked
to see the ammonite
shell. He frowned.

'Why is this on the
floor?' He gently picked
it up. 'Ruby, what's going
on? Where's Indie?'

I explained as quickly as I could.

'. . . and then I saw the study was UNLOCKED and the door was OPEN. I heard Little Indie roar, and there was a really STRANGE RUMBLING SOUND and a FLASH OF LIGHT, and –'

Dad gasped. 'Ruby . . . This is REALLY important – how many times did Little Indie ROAR?'

'Three times,' I said. 'I think . . .'

Dino Dad's eyes went REALLY wide. Then he made a very loud GULP, and his face went a slightly green colour.

'Oh, dear,' he said, as he started pacing round his study. 'Oh, deary, deary, dear.'

'What's wrong, Dad?'

Dad stopped pacing and looked at me.

'Ruby, I have to tell you something.'
Dad sounded SERIOUS. 'Your mum and
I were going to tell you all about this
when you were older, but I don't think we
can wait that long now . . .'

I was very CURIOUS and quiet. What
was he going to say?

'You see, Ruby . . . you're a POOPA.'
'**A POOPA?!**' I frowned and
gave a little giggle.

'A POOPA,' Dad said again. 'It
stands for PROTECTOR OF OUR
PREHISTORIC ALLIES.'

I was sure this must be one of Dad's
games. But he had his serious face on.

'You see this?' Dad picked up the
ammonite shell. 'It holds VERY SPECIAL

33

POWERS. Remember when I told you about how your great-great-great-grandad, William Thumb, found the shell many years ago?'

'Yes,' I said, nodding.

'When he found it, he took it back to his lab to study it. And he soon discovered

something amazing. If he roared three times in a row, the ammonite shell came alive . . . and with a FLASH and a RUMBLE and a WHOOSH, he was transported to an ISLAND – an island that had REAL-LIFE DINOSAURS living on it!'

I couldn't believe what I was hearing.

'So . . . you're saying there are dinosaurs still alive today?' I asked, confused. Maybe Dad had hit his head too hard while he was chasing Indie!

'YES, my Ruby Roo!' Dad said excitedly. 'Scientists think ALL dinosaurs became extinct, but they're wrong. Some MAGICALLY disappeared and reappeared on a SPECIAL island because of the power of this PREHISTORIC SHELL. Your great-great-great-grandad looked after all the dinosaurs he found – and now, Ruby, WE are the protectors of the island, which William named "Dinotropolis".'

'That's amazing, that's so exciting, I can't believe –' I paused. I'd had a sudden realization. 'Dad, that means Little Indie must have accidentally been transported to Dino-trop-a-poppa-lis, or whatever it's called!' I gasped. 'We've got to rescue her!'

'You're right! Come on, Ruby. It's time for a REAL adventure! Let me show you what us POOPAs can do,' said Dad.

'You mean . . . we're going there now?' I whooped.

'THAT'S RIGHT! Let's **gooooo!**'

Chapter 3
DINOTROPOLIS

Dino Dad jumped into action.
'We must rescue your sister and
bring her back here before your mum
gets home for tea, or there's a chance
she may be the tiniest bit cross with me,'
Dad said, knowing she was going to be
humongously cross with him.

He reached down and took my T.rex
head and feet off. 'You won't be needing
these, Ruby Dooby,' he smiled.

I grinned back at him. 'Are we REALLY going to Dino-trop-o-bus?'

'Yep!' Dino Dad put the ammonite shell back on the floor. 'Hold my hand, Ruby. It's going to seem a little strange at first, and you might feel a bit dizzy . . . but don't worry - your old Dino Dad is here.'

'I'm not scared,' I said (though I was maybe just a little bit nervous). 'I hope Indie's OK, though.'

'I'm sure she'll be fine,' Dad said. 'I'm more worried about everyone else!'

I squeezed Dad's hand.

'Right – ready? *ROAR . . .!*' said Dino Dad, and the ammonite shell's colours started to glow.

'*ROAR!*' Dad said again. This time, the colours started swirling around and getting brighter.

'Ready?' he whispered to me.

'Ready!'

'Then here we go . . . *ROAR!*' Dad shouted. A beam of bright light and colours filled the room, and a rumbling started below our feet. Suddenly, a

moving, swirling door shape appeared
in front of us. Then – *WHOOSH!* –
we were SUCKED into the door and
moving VERY, VERY fast, spinning as
we travelled. All around, I could see the
rainbow colours of the magic ammonite
shell – and what looked like the shadows
of lots of different dinosaurs. It was
amazing!

But something strange was happening. My arms felt a bit itchy – almost like they were growing. And my feet felt heavy. And . . . was it just me, or did it feel like my neck was stretching?

THWUMP! We landed.

Ooft! What a ride. It had been a bit bumpy, but we made it! I couldn't wait to take a look around Dinotropolis.

'Huh,' I heard Dad huff from behind me. 'Even after all these years, I STILL can't get used to the landing! Are you OK, Ruby?'

I stood up. I felt very DIZZY and WOBBLY on my feet. My sight was all blurry. I looked down at my body . . .

and I couldn't believe what I was seeing!

I had feathers on my arms, and my feet had three clawed toes on each side. My skin was all scaly, and I could feel something swishing behind me.

OMG! It was a tail!

I WAS A DINOSAUR!!

'Oh, fantastic! You're a Troodon, Ruby, and one of the smartest dinosaurs on Dinotropolis,' I heard Dino Dad say with pride.

43

I spun round – and was amazed all over again, because my dad wasn't my dad any more . . . he was a dinosaur, too!

His neck had grown really long, and his body had become much, MUCH bigger, with four massive legs, each ending in a massive foot. I looked at Dino Dad's now very different face . . . and I could still make out his smile. He also had his slightly curly and VERY HUGE mop of hair on top of his head – just like

normal Dad, only . . . dinosaur-y.

'And what kind of dino do you think your old dad is?'

'Erm . . . an Argentinosaurus?'
My eyes were bulging
as I looked up at
my huge
Dino Dad.

'YES!' Dad looked delighted. 'I'm one of the tallest dinosaurs around. It makes it hard for me to fit into most places, but it means I can see for MILES and keep an eye on everything on Dinotropolis.'

'Dad, that's great . . . but could you please explain a small, teeny-weeny, ever-so-tiny detail to me?'

'Of course,' Dad replied with a warm and eager smile.

'WHY didn't you tell me WE would become dinosaurs?!'

Dad's dino jaw dropped, and he slapped one of his great big feet on his forehead. Ouch!

That must have hurt!

'Oh my goodness, Ruby. Did I forget to mention this part?'

I nervously laughed. 'Just a bit!'

'Sorry, Rubes, I just got so excited about you finally knowing you were a POOPA that I completely forgot to tell you,' he said clumsily.

'Well, as you can see,

when we come to Dinotropolis, we become dinosaurs that are based on our natural characters, statures or strengths. For example, I'm very tall, so naturally, I'm a TALL dinosaur. Your mother is very caring and motherly, so she is a Maiasaura. And you're clearly VERY clever, because you, my Ruby, are a Troodon.'

'Mum is a Maiasaura?' I repeated with a wondering smile, trying to take it all in. 'So what was William Thumb when he arrived here? He must have had a bit of a shock.'

'Well.' Dad paused. 'He turned into *a T.REX*,' he said.

'A T.rex!' I replied with excitement.

'Yes, indeed, because he was a great leader, Ruby. Over many years, he taught the dinosaurs how to speak and live like us without wanting to EAT each other, too!'

'Wow!' *Well, that's pretty cool,* I thought. I'd always imagined what it would be like to be a dinosaur. But I was curious. 'How did he get all the CARNIVORES not to eat meat?'

'Blue coconuts,' Dad blurted out with a smile.

'Huh?'

'Blue coconuts, Ruby!' he said again. 'They have everything in them

that a dinosaur needs to please its belly and keep it strong,' Dino Dad said, ushering my eyes to the hundreds of blue-coconut trees on the island. 'And, as you can see, there's no shortage of blue coconuts on Dinotropolis.'

'**Ohhhhh**, so THAT'S where they come from!' I said, happy in the knowledge that I finally knew. *I can't believe I didn't guess that, for our whole lives, Mum and Dad were feeding us coconuts they picked from a secret island full of dinosaurs who could talk. I mean, it was so obvious!* I jokingly thought.

It was a lot to take in. *I WAS AN*

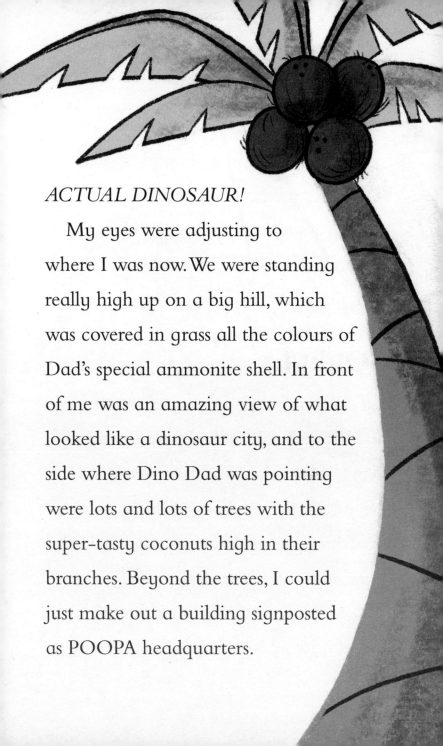

ACTUAL DINOSAUR!

My eyes were adjusting to
where I was now. We were standing
really high up on a big hill, which
was covered in grass all the colours of
Dad's special ammonite shell. In front
of me was an amazing view of what
looked like a dinosaur city, and to the
side where Dino Dad was pointing
were lots and lots of trees with the
super-tasty coconuts high in their
branches. Beyond the trees, I could
just make out a building signposted
as POOPA headquarters.

This is incredible, I thought.
Not long ago, I was playing
hide-and-seek with Indie, and now I was
a real-life dinosaur! Then I wondered: *if
Dad and I are dinosaurs, then is Indie one,
too?* What has SHE turned into?

It wouldn't be easy finding her,

that was for sure.

'Right, Dad. Let's go and look for –'

BBRRRR, BBRRRRRRR!

All of a sudden, an ear-splitting noise

rang out.

'Goodness! That's the warning

alarm,' Dino Dad said.

The ground started to shake. What could be causing that?

Then I saw it! Running towards us with stompy feet and a GIANT head was a HUGE, rather worried-looking T.rex. He wore black glasses and a blue shirt

with a badge on it – and just behind him I could see a smaller T.rex, wearing a cap that read I LOVE POOPAs.

The big T.rex reached us first and seemed quite out of breath.

'C-c-code red, Lionel! It's a code red! There's a dinosaur causing complete chaos here on DINOTROPOLIS – it's like they don't know how to behave like a civilized dinosaur at all!'

Dino Dad's face dropped. Then he turned to me. 'Uh oh, Ruby! I think we've found Little Indie!'

Chapter 4
STANLEY AND REX

I stepped back with my huge new Troodon feet, a little wary of the T.rex.

'It's a total e-roar-gency, Lionel! The dino on the loose is causing complete carnivore carnage!'

The T.rex seemed nervous, but also harmless, so I relaxed a bit.

'Calm down, Stanley,' Dad said. 'I'm pretty sure the dinosaur you're talking about is Little Indie, my daughter. She

escaped through the magic shell! We're here to find her and get her back home before she causes a kerfuffle!'

'T-t-too late for that, Lionel! She's already been to Mrs Docus's Prehistoric Nursery for Diddy Dinos and made quite the scene, I'm afraid.'

'Ah,' Dino Dad replied. 'Sounds like our Indie! Have you got the coordinates for where she is now?'

'No, I'm sorry – Indie knocked over our radar! The whole system is down.'

Wow! Indie really is causing chaos, I thought, as I watched the two huge dinosaurs talking.

'Crikey,' said Dad. 'Well, in that case, we'll just have to follow her trail of destruction.'

Stanley looked relieved – then finally noticed me.

'Hello! Who's this, Lionel?'

'Hi! I'm –'

'Ruby Thumb!' interrupted the small T.rex wearing the POOPAs cap.

'Erm, yes,' I said, 'that's me!' How did he know who I was?

'Lovely to meet you, Ruby!' The big T.rex smiled and tried to shake my claw, but realized his arms were too short. Whoops! 'Is this your other daughter, Lionel? You should have said! It's a pleasure to m–m–meet you. A Troodon, I see! Lionel, you were right. I owe you a coconut!'

'Ha, yes, you do, old friend! Ruby, this is Stanley. He's my right-hand dino. Stanley looks after things on Dinotropolis when I'm not here.' He leaned down and whispered, 'And sometimes he can be a bit stressy . . .!'

'Hey, I h-h-heard that!' Stanley adjusted his glasses, clearly a bit miffed. 'I'll have you know there's always a lot to do around here, especially when your dad is off having a D-D-Dino-Dad Day with you and Indie.'

Now the smaller T.rex stepped forward to say hello. 'Hi, I'm Rex. I'm kind of a fan of yours – well, actually, of all humans! What's it like where you live? What's it like to be human? Do you eat with a knife and fork?!'

'Now, Rex, don't bombard her with questions. She's only just arrived!' said Stanley. 'He's fascinated with all things h-h-human, Ruby. He's my son and has wanted to meet you for a long time.'

'Oh, that's OK!' I said happily. 'Nice to meet you, Rex. It's great being human, but not as great as it is being a dinosaur!' I smiled, and Rex smiled back.

'Right! Now that we're all introduced, we really MUST look for your sister!' Dino Dad said. 'First stop: Mrs Docus's Prehistoric Nursery for Diddy Dinos.'

'She wasn't best pleased, Lionel,' said Stanley, sounding worried again. 'You know how strict she is. She used to terrify me when I was taught by her!'

'Don't worry, Stanley. We'll be fine,' said Dad bravely. 'You two concentrate on getting that radar back online!'

'Right-o, Lionel, will do! Come on, Rex.' Stanley saluted.

'Nice to meet you, Ruby!' said Rex, waving at me.

'And you! Good luck!' I called back.

Rex left with a skip in his stomp alongside his dad, both making the ground shake again as they ran.

Dino Dad turned towards me. 'Want to know a shortcut?' He grinned, and then stretched his long neck down the side of the hill, like a slide. 'Slide on down, Ruby Roo!'

He didn't need to ask me twice! I hopped up on to Dad's neck and let go. '**Wheeeeeeeeeee!**'

I screamed as I sped really fast down Dad's massive Argentinosaurus neck. I carried on sliding all the way down

63

the hill, until I finally came to a stop at the bottom.

'THAT WAS AMAZING!' I said, as I got up and brushed my dusty dino-bum clean.

Beep beep!

What was that? I turned just in time to see Dino Dad coming between the trees in a car that was just a little bit too small for him. It screeched to a stop right in front of me.

'To the nursery!' Dad yelled, pointing in that direction – and off we went!

Chapter 5
CAKEY CHAOS

We arrived outside Mrs Docus's Nursery to a terrible amount of noise, including some raucous roaring giggles from inside.

Dad and I jumped out of the car and raced towards the open front door. Then, all of a sudden, **SPLAT!**

A piece of coconut cream cake splattered into Dad's face.

'Oooooh! You diddy doughnuts, stop

that right now! That's not funny!' came
a shout.

We went inside and could see all the
diddy dinos racing around, having what
looked like a cake fight! It really was
carnage. There was cake everywhere – on
all the books, the chairs and
the windows, too!

At the far end of
the classroom was
Mrs Deirdre Docus –
a well-dressed, slightly
older-looking Diplodocus. She wore
glasses and had a thick, decorative scarf
tied round her neck, and her very long tail
was swishing in annoyance as she tried to
wrangle the diddy dinos.

'Settle down, everyone!'
She spotted Dad. 'Oh,
Lionel, my deepest
apologies – there is
not usually such
disorder in here!
As you can see, it's
complete chaos.'

'Don't worry, Mrs Docus,' Dad said,
wiping his face. 'Tastes delicious!'

'Wow! There's so
much cream flying
around it looks
like it's snowing!'
I said.

'THANK
YOU, young
lady. But I'll have
you know we've NEVER
had SNOW on Dinotropolis,'
Mrs Docus huffed back at me.

'Oh,' I said sheepishly. 'Sorry.'
It looked like Stanley had been right
about her being strict! But she was soon
distracted by someone else.

'CARLY CARNOTAURUS! Put that down!' Mrs Docus bellowed over the noise of the classroom.

Another piece of cream cake came flying towards her, and she used her long tail to swipe it away – right in the direction of Dino Dad!

SPLAT!

Now he was covered in twice the cream!

Dad calmly licked his face with his giant tongue, and I giggled under my breath.

'This is a disaster, Lionel!' Mrs Docus
shouted above the din of the rampaging
diddy dinos. 'We were having a lovely,
calm time before this started. I was
reading them *The Allosaurus Who
Came to Tea,* and then, all of a sudden,
a cheeky diddy dino shot into the
classroom, grabbed Valerie Velociraptor's
coconut cream birthday cakes and started
throwing them around! Before I knew it,

the whole classroom had joined in, and I haven't been able to calm them down since,' she said, her voice peaking to a wail.

'OK – what did this particular diddy dino look like, Mrs Docus?' Dad asked, ducking his head as more cream cakes were thrown about.

'I didn't see! It was very fast – and, in case you hadn't noticed, I had a bunch of screaming, roaring, cake-throwing dinosaurs running around!' came her reply.

'Sorry to hear that, Mrs Docus.' Dad paused. 'I can see you're not keen on the s-CREAMING!' Dino Dad chuckled and winked at me.

Mrs Docus didn't look impressed. 'It's no joking matter, Lionel! This wouldn't have happened in my day!'

'Erm, yes, of course.' Dino Dad quickly moved on. 'We're trying to track the rampaging dinosaur down. We think it's my daughter. She's on the loose –'

'Oh, I see! The dino is YOUR daughter, is she? So this is YOUR doing, then?' Mrs Docus said.

Uh oh! Dino Dad was in for a telling off now!

'Well, yes . . . she's normally a very quiet child!' Dad said. I quickly covered up my laugh, but Dad gave me A Look. 'Never fear, Mrs Docus – we'll find her and clean this mess up, I promise!'

'HUH.' Mrs Docus huffed. And as she turned – **SPLAT!** – another flying cake hit her right on the chin. It made her look like she had a cake beard!

I suddenly realized something.

'Dad, if Mrs Docus couldn't SEE this diddy dinosaur, she must have been VERY speedy. So Little Indie must have turned into a really FAST dinosaur.'

'Maybe, Ruby Roo,' said Dino Dad. 'That might narrow it down a bit!'

Just then a massive

CRASH came from

behind us. Somehow, the room

was getting even more rowdy!

'I think we'd better help,

Dad,' I said.

'Yes, yes, of course,' replied Dino

Dad. 'I'll get this sorted out in two tiny

ticks!' He stepped forward.

'Now listen up, little ones! I know

you're having fun, but Mrs Docus has told

you to stop, so all of you just put down

your cakes and –'

SPLAT! **SPLAT!** *SPLAT!*
SPLAT! SPLAT!

Dad was sooo covered in cream cakes

now that you could only see his eyeballs!

He looked like a giant cake monster!

I had to help. How were we going to get the attention of these rowdy roarers? Suddenly, I had another light-bulb moment.

'Dad, I've got it! What do you and Mum always do when you want to get our attention?'

Dino Dad thought for a second. 'Well, we do the pop-pop dance.'

'Exactly,' I said. 'Let's give it a try!'

The pop-pop dance is brilliant – it's basically Mum and Dad making fart sounds from their armpits while wiggling around. It always makes me and Indie laugh. It's VERY funny.

Dino Dad lifted his big foot to reach

under his armpit and squelched down, but no sound came out.

'Oh, dear – it's a bit harder to make the pop-pop sounds with these big dino feet, Ruby Roo . . . but don't worry. Your old Dino Dad has an idea.' And with that, he started licking up all the cake cream from his face.

'Cover your ears, everyone. . . and your nose!' Then he lifted his tail and let out a big, loud, real-life, dino-size pop-pop! Then he began stomping and popping around the room.

The diddy dinos stopped in their tracks and fell about laughing.

'It's working!' I said, covering my nose.

Deirdre Docus was in total shock.

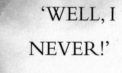

'WELL, I
NEVER!'
she said.
Now we
had their attention, I
swooped in to take over.

'Copy me, everyone!' I said, starting
to dance. The diddy dinos joined in,
and then after a few seconds I stopped
dancing, and they stopped, too. I put my
claws in the air, and they copied me. Then
I sat down quietly on the floor – and
guess what? So did they.

'We did it!' I said, feeling pleased with

myself. 'Even if it was a bit stinky . . .'

Mrs Docus took a breath, then wiped her face and glasses with a giant tissue. 'Right, class, now we've got that out of our system, let's get this place cleaned up! And Lionel – good luck finding your daughter! Try to teach her to behave with more decorum next time, please.'

Dino Dad smiled awkwardly at Mrs Docus, then gave me a nod to go. But just as we were about to leave, I noticed some cakey footprints leading out of the nursery's back door.

'Dad! Look.' I pointed to the floor.

'Footprints! Well spotted, Ruby Roo.'
He looked at them closely. 'Hmm. Three
toes and very small, bird-like footprints –
I would say Little Indie is a carnivore,
for sure.'

'I agree,' I said. 'Let's gather the
evidence. We know that she's fast, she's
small and she's probably a carnivore. But
which one?'

We both thought for a second, then
with a smile Dino Dad and I looked at
each other and both said at the same time:

'A Compsognathus!'

I remembered Dad doing a talk at
his museum about 'Compys'. They were
very quick and had great eyesight, which
wouldn't help us if Indie still thought we
were playing hide-and-seek – she might
see us coming from far away and go and
hide again!

We'd have to be clever.

'Follow those footprints!' said
Dino Dad.

Chapter 6
DINO-LYMPIC GAMES

We began following the creamy footprints, but it wasn't long before they ran out. We kept looking, but it was really hard not to get distracted – Dinotropolis was full of amazing sights!

As we walked further, I began to hear some very loud cheering close to where we were.

'What's that, Dad?'

'Ah!' he said. 'That'll be the annual

Dino-lympic Games! Every year, we bring together brilliant sports-dinosaurs to compete. Usually I give out the awards, but this year's event fell on a Dino-Dad Day, and obviously I wasn't going to miss that.'

'Aww, thanks, Dad,' I said.

We heard another big cheer from the crowd. That gave me an idea. 'Dad! Indie loves big, noisy places! What if she went into the stadium?'

Dad beamed. 'You could be right, Ruby Roobster! Let's take a look. There will be a lot of dinos in there, so it won't be easy to find a small Compy like Little Indie. Keep your eyes open!'

We made our way towards the stadium,

and it wasn't long before we were at the entrance. Inside, I could see it was full of hundreds of dinosaurs, all cheering and supporting their favourite sports stars!

Everywhere I looked, amazing games were going on.

'It's the ski jump!' said Dad, pointing over to one area of the stadium. 'Fantastic sport. The Microraptors usually compete in that one – they slide down the Diplodocuses' necks!'

Suddenly, we heard a voice booming over the speaker. 'Prehistoric friends, dinos, Pterosaurs and fans of . . . ME!!

Ha ha ha, just kidding!'

A huge Brachiosaurus wearing a smart
suit jacket and sunglasses was standing
in the centre of the stadium with a
microphone.

'Who's that, Dad?' I asked.

'Hmm, that's Barry Bracho. He's
the main host for live events here on
Dinotropolis. He can be a bit full
of himself, but he's a great
public speaker!'

'All-righty, righty, righty, rumble! THE TIME HAS COME to introduce our speedy dino pals to the start line for the main event: THE SUPER SPRINT!'

From the side of the racetrack, four dinosaurs made their way forward, waving at the crowd.

'In lane one, we've got the two-time Dinotropolis champion – give her a cheer and an old-time ROAR: it's Vicky Vello, the Velociraptor!'

The stadium got very loud as Vicky jogged to her lane, warming up as she went.

'In lane two, please give a massive cheer for Timmy "The Tornado" T.rex!'

Timmy moved his tiny arms up and

down as he ran to his lane. Immediately, the crowd started copying him. It looked like they were all doing doggy paddle!

'Ha ha, that's our Timmy!' Barry laughed and copied Timmy's arm movements, too.

Dad must have seen how confused I was, as he leaned down to explain. 'It's his signature move,' he said. 'The crowd love it!'

'Finally, in lanes three and four, let's give a warm welcome back to the reigning champions: the SPINOSAURUS SISTERS!'

The crowd whooped, cheered and roared as the two sisters made their way to their lanes. They were both dressed exactly the same, but with different-coloured bows on their heads to tell them apart.

As the dinos were getting into position, from the corner of my eye I saw another dinosaur running towards the track.

It was much smaller, had bird-like feet, very familiar hair – AND it was covered in cream cake. IT MUST BE . . .

'LITTLE INDIE!' I shouted to Dino Dad. 'LOOK!'

Dad saw her, too. 'So it is! Well spotted, Ruby. Let's try and get her over here without anyone noticing,' he half

whispered. 'I'd rather not
have everyone know it's my
daughter who's been on the rampage!'

'LITTLE INDIE!' I yelled.

'Or we can just shout her name,' Dino
Dad said, rolling his eyes.

'Sorry, Dad – but we're running out of
time! We have to get home before Mum
gets back!' I told him.

'Good point! OH, ALL RIGHT –
LITTLE INDIE!' he joined in.

Amazingly – even though there was a
lot of noise in the stadium – Little Indie

seemed to hear us. She turned around and smiled . . . but the smile was a cheeky-looking one. Even though she was now a dinosaur, I knew what that cheeky smile meant!

'*ROAR, ROAR!*' she yelled with gusto.

'Uh oh – Dad, I reckon she thinks we're going to CHASE her!'

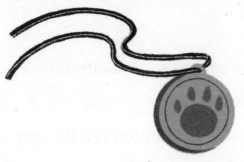

Chapter 7
THE BIG RACE

'Oh, deary, deary, dear,' said Dino Dad, knowing I was probably right.

The race was about to begin!

'On your marks! Claws ready! GO!' yelled Barry Bracho.

The dino racers leapt off their marks, and the race was on! With one mini addition . . .

Indie the Compy ran alongside the

dino athletes at super speed, ROARING
and smiling as she went.

There was only one thing I could
do – I had to catch her! I sped towards the
track, moving my new dino feet as fast as
I could. And I was moving VERY fast!

'And they're off! The Spinosaurus sisters
have started with a real stomp, but Vicky
Vello the Velociraptor isn't far behind, and
Timmy T.rex, who is stomping just behind
her, BUT . . . HANG ON A MINUTE!
Who is this new contender?! It's . . . it's a
Compsognathus! She's only a youngster,
but, wow, look how fast she is.'

Indie was now overtaking Timmy T.rex.
But I was moving fast, too, and soon I was
on the track as well.

'**NOW** what's happening?! A
Troodon has also joined the race! What
an exciting twist. . . and let me tell you,
everyone, she is certainly in it to win it
with that turn of speed . . .'

The crowd were on their feet, cheering

and whooping!

'The Compy is just ahead . . . Oh, but what's this? The Troodon has made a last-minute LEAP over the finish line at the same time as the Compy . . . IT'S A DRAW!'

As I leapt, I tried to grab hold of Indie, but she slipped through my claws and carried on running out of the stadium. She was laughing away, still thinking this was all a big game!

PHEW! I lay on the floor, completely
out of breath!

'What an amazing race!' Barry
continued, the crowd still cheering.
'Though, oh dear, Timmy doesn't look
too happy! But who were the amazing
new competitors?'

Dino Dad rushed down and took the
microphone from Barry. 'A-hem!' he said,

trying to get the crowd to quiet down.

'Actually, I know who the new racers are . . .' he said, half embarrassed and half proud. 'They are my daughters, Ruby –' He pointed to me – 'and Indie!'

The crowd went silent and then ERUPTED INTO APPLAUSE!

Barry swiped the mic back from Dino Dad.

'WHAT? That's incredible – what a twist to these amazing Dino-lympic Games! We have two new super-sprint champions – the POOPA SISTERS . . .!'

Dad grabbed the mic back from Barry and interrupted. 'Erm – actually, I would prefer the THUMB sisters, if you don't mind . . .'

Barry rolled his eyes and took the mic once again. 'All right then, the Thumb sisters – champions of the super sprint! And now, my dino friends, that's it for the Dino-lympic Games this year, but don't go anywhere! Next up, we have a special performance from HERBIE AND THE LEAFEATERS to close the games!'

And the crowd gave another massive ROAR!

Chapter 8
HERBIE AND THE LEAFEATERS

I made my way over to Dino Dad, who picked me up and hugged me.

'Well done, Ruby Roo – what a race!'

'Thanks, Dad – but Indie ran off again! She slipped through my claws,' I said, feeling downbeat.

'You tried your hardest, Ruby. Don't worry – I'll make

sure we get your sister back in time for Mum coming home,' he reassured me. 'Because if we don't, I think I might be sleeping in the shed tonight . . .'

I chuckled, but that didn't solve our problem. How could we get Little Indie to come to us?

1. Build a huge net and trick her into it with some incredibly tasty dinosaur-shaped baby biscuits?

2. Invent a mini Compy robot toy to befriend her and talk her into coming back home?

3. Somehow just try to tell her the game of hide-and-seek is over?

Hmm, all too obvious, I thought.

Just then, I heard a loud voice not too far from us, whooping, 'FUN, FUN, FUN!' I looked over and saw it was a Centrosaurus – I recognized the big frill on its neck from Dad's museum – and she was guiding a band towards the stage with their instruments.

'Ooh, it's Serena! She's in charge of fun

and festivities on Dinotropolis,' said Dino Dad, who waved her over.

'Helloooo, Lionel!' said Serena. 'And helloooo, Ruby! I saw the race – you are suuuuper whizzy-fast! You and your sister are true champions!' Serena looked around for Indie. 'Where is your other little speedy lizard, Lionel?'

'Well,' said Dad, looking sheepish. 'Our little Compy has disappeared again ...'

'Oh, no! She might miss Herbie and the Leafeaters! Music is food for the soul on Dinotropolis,' Serena wailed dramatically.

'I thought you all ate COLOURFUL COCONUTS?' I asked.

'I think what Serena means is that music makes us feel good, Ruby Roo,'

Dino Dad explained with a warm smile. 'Isn't that right?'

Herbie was the coolest-looking Triceratops I'd ever seen! Not that I had seen many up until now. She had blue ribbons on each horn and a jean jacket

with a sparkly 'H' on the pocket. She seemed to be the lead singer of the band, and I liked her straight away!

'Abso-dino-lutely!' she replied, smiling at me. 'Music is what makes us ROAR on the inside, Ruby.'

I returned her smile. Then, suddenly, I had an idea!

'THAT'S IT!!' I yelled. 'Herbie, can I give you a song request, please?'

She laughed. 'Of course! You're the race champion, and a special one at that.'

I reached up to whisper in Herbie's ear. She gave me a nod, then went to tell the rest of the band the song.

'What did you ask for, Ruby Roo?' Dino Dad asked.

'Well, what's the one thing that Little Indie always comes running for when she hears it?'

He thought for a second, then realized. 'Ruby, you are brilliant – her Roaring Nursery-Rhyme Dino's song!'

'Exactly! I asked Herbie to play that, but maybe with a bit more ROCK…!'

Barry Bracho stepped up to the microphone again.

'Carnivores, herbivores and those in-between-ivores! Let's hear it for Herbie and the Leafeaters!'

'One, two, three, four! *ROAR . . . ROAR . . . R-ROAR . . . ROAR . . . ROAR . . . R-ROAR . . .!*' Herbie began

singing. The whole band started rocking out, and everyone in the stadium got to their feet and began dancing! Even Dino Dad was jumping and twirling round.

I danced, too, but was also keeping an eye out for Little Indie. I couldn't see her anywhere, but then, on the other side of the stadium, moving pretty quickly towards us was a COMPY, wiggling her tail-y bum to the beat. I'd have known that bum wiggle anywhere.

'INDIE!!' I shouted.

My plan had worked!

Dad and I gave her a big hug, then started wiggling our bums, too – even though Dad's giant bum kept bumping into things!

'ROAR... ROARRRRRRRRR!'

Herbie ended the song with a really long roar, and the stadium exploded into cheers and whoops. I gave Herbie a 'claws-up', and she nodded and smiled back!

Then Dino Dad swooped my sister up on to his back.

'Right, you cheeky thing! You're staying put with me.'

Serena shouted up to Dad, 'Stay until

the end of the gig, Lionel! Don't forget: fun, fun, FUN!'

He looked at his watch. 'Well –'

'**PLEE**E**AASS**S**E**E**?**' I said.

'Oh, all right then!' Dino Dad laughed. 'I guess we have what we came for!' He looked down at Little Indie.

'*ROAR!*' she said.

Chapter 9
HOME FOR TEA

When the gig was over, it was finally time to say goodbye to everyone. The crowd chanted, 'Thumb sisters! Thumb sisters!' while wiggling their bums, which was now OUR signature move, apparently!

We hugged Serena and the band, and with Little Indie finally found, we headed off home.

As we approached Mrs Docus's Nursery

again, we could hear some VERY LOUD SNORING coming from inside. I poked my head in to see all of the diddy dinos and Mrs Docus fast asleep, still with cake everywhere! I smiled, and – using my new Troodon super speed – I raced around, quickly clearing everything up.

'That should please Mrs Docus!' I said.

'Well done, Ruby Roo,' Dino Dad said, giving me a pat on the shoulder.

It was only a short drive to the POOPA headquarters, where the magic shell portal was waiting for us. I was so happy to see Stanley and Rex there.

'H-h-hello, Lionel! And Ruby – the radar is up and working again, but I'm guessing it's not needed now,' Stanley greeted us. 'Why, hello, Little Indie!' He seemed more relaxed and gave Little Indie a smile. 'We s-s-saw you both at the stadium – very impressive! And I look forward to seeing more of you here on Dinotropolis!'

'Oh, YES, PLEASE!' I replied.

'All right then, team, it's definitely time to go! Your mum will be home very soon – and we can have some yummy blue-coconut curry. I'm hungry!' said Dino Dad, rubbing his tummy.

'Me, too,' I said, licking my lips. Indie gave a tiny tired and hungry roar.

'I have something for you, Ruby,' Rex said, and he handed me a piece of paper with something on it. 'I thought

I would draw
a picture
of you and
your sister winning
the race. I've signed it, too!'

'WOW! Thanks, Rex! That is really
kind of you!' The drawing was amazing!
'This is the best present I've ever had.' I
gave him a hug. 'Maybe next time I'll
bring you something from where I live.'

Rex beamed at the thought. 'Yes,
please, Ruby!'

Then, finally, it was time to go
home. We turned to face the magic
ammonite-shell portal.

'Together?' Dino Dad asked with a grin.

'One each,' I said.

Dad started with a low '*ROAR*', and the ammonite began to glow.

I did the second '*ROAR*' a bit louder.

Then, '*ROAR!!*' said Little Indie, and with that there was a huge beam of bright light. Swirling colours filled the air in front of us, and the ground began to rumble underneath our feet. A moving, swirling door appeared and – *WHOOSH!* – we were sucked through!

As we spun, my claws changed back to normal feet and hands, my feathers disappeared and my head began

changing back to my normal Ruby head.
I could see Dino Dad and Little Indie
changing, too, until – *THWUMP!* We
were safely home in Dad's office.

'Oh, I already miss being a
Troodon,' I said, looking
at my hands and
touching my face.
At least I still had
the picture Rex
had drawn for
me. 'What an
adventure! What
a Dino-Dad Day
it's been. When
can we go back?'
Dino Dad laughed.

117

'Woah, woah, woah, Ruby Roo! If we don't get everything tidied up before your mum comes home – and if she even gets the slightest WHIFF of where we've been today – then you won't be going back for a while! Come on, my dino divas. Operation Tidy-Up is go!'

The dinosaur costumes we'd been wearing earlier were still on the floor, so we picked them up and put them back

on. '*ROAR!*' said Little Indie, and she sped off into the kitchen. Dad and I followed

(Dad hit his Velociraptor head on the door again – oops!).

In the kitchen, there was still some porridge on the cupboards and floor. I put down my special picture, picked up a cloth and started cleaning it up, while Dad turned on the oven to pop in Mum's blue-coconut curry.

'I'm not sure anyone would believe us if I told them where we get our blue coconuts from!' I laughed, and so did Dino Dad.

Dad patted my T.rex head, and as he did we heard keys jingling at the front door. It was six o'clock on the dot. Mum was home!

The front door opened, and Indie and

I went running to see her. 'Hello, Thumb family – Mummy's home! How are my sweet girls?' Mum laughed as she put her coat on her hook and her cameras on the floor. 'Ooooh, I missed you all today!' she said, kissing our heads. 'And you, you big tree,' she said to Dino Dad, and stood on her tiptoes to give him a kiss.

'How were the beavers?' Dino Dad asked.

'Oh, they were tricky to find,' Mum replied. 'It was like they were playing a giant game of hide-and-seek!'

Eek! Just like us and Little Indie!

Dino Dad looked at me and made a secret '*SHH!*' noise!

'But, more importantly, my lovelies,

how was Dino-Dad Day?'

'Well . . .' I said, 'I think it was one of the best Dino-Dad Days EVER!'

'Oh, yes!' Dad replied. 'It was FUN, FUN, FUN, wasn't it, Ruby Roo?'

'*ROAR!*' Little Indie agreed.

'Oh, I'm so glad. Now, who wants some curry?'

As we went back into the kitchen, I breathed a sigh of relief. I DESPERATELY wanted to tell Mum what had happened, but I knew I had to keep our adventure secret. At least for now, we had got away with it. Or had we?

'Ooooh, what's this? Has someone been doing some drawing?' Mum reached down to the chair she had just gone to sit on, and pulled up . . . my special picture!

'UH OH!' I said.

Mum looked at it . . . then at me and my sister . . . then back at the picture. She slowly raised her head towards Dino Dad.

'Lionel . . .?! I think we might need to have a little chat!' Mum calmly said with a sort of gritted-teethy pretend smile.

'Now, now, Belinda! Remember – you're the pastry to my cream cake! Let's not lose our tempers . . .!' Dad said nervously. 'Indie was only lost on Dinotropolis for a little while!'

'LIONEL!'

Dad zipped away from Mum, but she
chased in him a circle round the table,
Dad bashing his Velociraptor head on the
light as he ran.

'My sweetness!' – *BASH!* – 'Let me
explain' – *BASH!* – 'I'm sure you'll
see the funny side eventually!' – *BASH!*
Dad pleaded.

Little Indie and I giggled and roared as we watched our parents run around the kitchen.

What a strange but brilliant day this has been, I thought. *I can't WAIT to do it all again soon!*

So now you know our family secret . . . We're **POOPAs** – Protectors Of Our Prehistoric Allies!

And that was my first adventure on Dinotropolis. But it was definitely NOT my last!

I'll see you on our next adventure for some more amazing prehistoric fun!

RUBY'S DINO FACTS

🐚 It was actually William Buckland, a real palaeontologist (someone who studies fossils), who was the first person to write about a dinosaur called a Megalosaurus – and, yes, he named it, too.

🐚 The first person to discover a dinosaur bone was Robert Plot, an English naturalist (an expert in natural history), but he didn't know what it was at the time!

It was Richard Owen, a British palaeontologist, who came up with the word 'dinosaur', meaning 'terrible lizard'.

A theropod was a type of two-legged, meat-eating dinsosaur.

The Troodon was one of the fastest dinosaurs, and one of the smartest.

The Compsognathus was also a smart and very quick dinosaur, and one of the smallest, too.

The Argentinosaurus is the second- largest dinosaur ever discovered . . . so far!

ACKNOWLEDGEMENTS

I would love to say a few thank yous to those who have helped make this book possible:

The team at Puffin for taking the chance on me and giving me such support along the way.

My brilliant editor, Naomi Colthurst, who ignited the idea of *Dino Dad*, and who has been such a positive force, working with my strengths and weaknesses to make writing my first book such an enjoyable experience.

130

Steven Lenton, whose fantastic artwork has brought this whole book to life better than I could have imagined.

My awesome agent, Craig Latto, who has always got my back and encourages me when it's needed and lets me be when I need time. (He is a very patient man!) He also introduced me to my other awesome (literary) agent, KT, who has simply been the best person to work with and has looked after me when it's been needed.

Everyone at the BBC, who gave me my dream of being an adventurer and who fuelled my boyhood passion for natural history and the prehistoric world in particular.

My legendary (hilarious) parents, Ian and Pippa Day, who are always so supportive and loving, and who definitely need their own TV show.

The lovely staff at Loaf in Bristol (where most of this book was written) for getting me endless amounts of delicious cake, sausage rolls and coffee to keep me going.

My beautiful kids for being a huge inspiration behind writing *Dino Dad* and who make me so proud every day.

My incredible wife, Kat, who is the best mother to our little ones and who has been nothing but an amazing support, both when I was writing this book and in everything I do. As Lionel Thumb would say to Belinda, 'You are the dressing to my salad.'

And finally, to the audience who have grown up with me and those who continue to watch me on children's TV, I wouldn't be able to do these things if it wasn't for you lovely lot, whose imaginations and innocence keep the child flourishing in all of us!

Look out for Dino Dad's
next adventure!

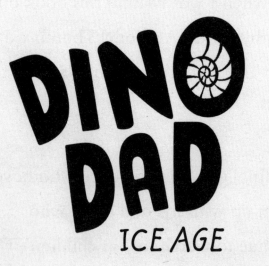

ICE AGE

Coming October 2024

What would you and your family look like in Dinotropolis?

Draw yourselves on these pages!